# #5 POKÉMON junior™

Adapted by **S. E. Heller**

SCHOLASTIC INC.
New York  Toronto  London  Auckland  Sydney
Mexico City  New Delhi  Hong Kong

ISBN 0-439-15431-6

Published by Scholastic Inc. All rights reserved.
SCHOLASTIC and associated logos are trademarks
and/or registered trademarks of Scholastic Inc.

Designed by Joan Moloney

12 11 10 9 8 7 6 5 4 3 2 1          0 1 2 3 4 5 6/0

Printed in the U.S.A.
First Scholastic printing, June 2000

## CHAPTER ONE

### A Trap Is Set

Pikachu and Ash were looking at a map. The two friends were traveling on the Orange Islands.

Pikachu loved Ash. And Ash loved Pikachu. The Lightning Mouse Pokémon and its trainer had been together for a long time. They were partners and good

friends. Ash wanted to become the world's greatest Pokémon trainer. And Pikachu wanted to help him!

"This island is full of Pidgeot and Rhydon," Tracey said. Tracey was another one of Ash's friends. Ash, Tracey, and another friend, Misty, traveled around together.

Pikachu looked worried. The flying

4

Pidgeot and the fierce Rhydon Pokémon looked like giants on this island.

"The Pokémon are big because they have a lot to eat," said Tracey.

"*Pika, pika,*" said Pikachu as the friends began to walk. *I wish there were lots of food for me!*

Suddenly, Ash stopped. Pikachu's eyes lit up! There was a big basket of fruit on the road right in front of them! Pikachu and Ash dashed toward it.

"Wait!" cried Misty. "Something is not right."

Ash and Pikachu still wanted to eat the fruit. Misty and Tracey did not agree.

"I think it is a trap," Misty said. "Fruit does not grow that way."

"But it is just sitting there," said Ash.

"*Pika pi,*" said Pikachu. *Yeah!*

Misty pointed to an apple tree by the side of the road. "We should eat these apples instead."

Ash, Pikachu, and Tracey followed her to the tree. Then, all of the sudden, they fell through the ground!

*Crash!* The friends had fallen into a hole.

Pikachu was surprised. It looked at Ash. An apple fell from the tree onto Ash's head. He tried to bite it. But it was really a stone! They had been tricked!

"Prepare for trouble," a voice

said from up above.

"Make it double," said another voice. It was Jessie and James, Team Rocket!

Pikachu knew that Team Rocket was up to no good. The two teenagers were always following Ash and his friends. They wanted to steal Pikachu.

"We put that basket on the ground to trick you," said Jessie. "We knew you would go to the tree instead. And you did!"

Pikachu looked at Ash. He was angry about being tricked.

# CHAPTER TWO

## Stuck Together!

"See?" Ash said to Misty. "We could have been eating. But no! You think too much."

"I cannot believe you are blaming me!" yelled Misty.

Pikachu did not want Ash and Misty to fight. They needed to beat Team Rocket together.

"Go, Arbok!" cried Jessie. Her Pokémon appeared from its Poké Ball. It looked like a big snake.

"Go, Weezing!" cried James. Weezing looked like a black cloud with two heads.

Ash looked at Pikachu. It was ready to fight. "I am counting on you, Pikachu," said Ash.

Pikachu wanted to make Ash proud. It sprang out of the hole.

"*Pika-chuu!*" It blasted Team Rocket with an Electric Shock. But Jessie, James, and Meowth, their talking Pokémon, had a

shield made
of rubber. It
blocked Electric
Attacks!

Arbok attacked Pikachu with its
Poison Sting. Weezing attacked
Pikachu with its Poison Gas.
Pikachu was hurt!

"*Pikaaa!*" cried Pikachu.

"Now!" cried Meowth.

Meowth ran to Pikachu and
locked a belt around it. The
talking Pokémon had a belt, too.
A cord connected the two belts.
Pikachu was attached to Meowth!

"Now Pikachu cannot get away from me!" yelled Meowth. Team Rocket grabbed Pikachu and dashed away.

Ash, Misty, and Tracey were still climbing out of the hole. They were too late!

"Pikachu!" shouted Ash.

## CHAPTER THREE

### A Giant Pidgeot

"We did it!" Meowth laughed.

"*Pika-chuu!*" Pikachu was very mad. It blasted Team Rocket. But they held up their shields.

"See? It does not work," Meowth told Pikachu. "You cannot hurt us now."

James and Jessie laughed. "We

have finally captured Pikachu!"
they said. "Now we can take him
to the boss."

But just then, something
stopped them. It was a giant
Pidgeot, and it was flying right at
them!

*Swoop!*

Team Rocket
tried to get away.
But Pidgeot grabbed
the cord that connected Pikachu
and Meowth. As they were lifted
into the air, Meowth's shield fell.

"Oh, no!" cried Meowth. Now it was not safe from Pikachu.

In fact, Meowth was not safe at all! Pidgeot flapped its giant wings. Up, up, up they went.

"I finally catch Pikachu and look what happens to me!" cried Meowth.

Pidgeot flew faster. Soon they would be at its nest.

"Do something, Pikachu!" cried Meowth.

"*Pikachuuu!*" cried the little yellow Pokémon. An Electric Shock blasted Meowth.

"Not me!" cried Meowth. "Get Pidgeot!"

Pikachu smiled. *"Pikachuuu!"* It blasted the Pidgeot. Pidgeot could not hold on. Pikachu's Electric Attack was too strong. It let go of the two Pokémon.

"Help!" cried Meowth. The two Pokémon were falling fast. It was a long way down.

*"Pika!"* cried Pikachu. It grabbed on to Meowth.

Meowth pushed Pikachu toward the ground. "I am not going to break your fall, Pikachu," it said.

16

The Pokémon flipped each other over. First Meowth was on top. Then Pikachu was on top.

*Crash!* The two Pokémon landed with a bang.

*"Pika!"* said Pikachu happily. Meowth did break its fall, after all!

# CHAPTER FOUR

## Meowth's Big Idea

"We have to go this way!"
Meowth ordered Pikachu.

"*Pika, pika!*" yelled Pikachu,
pulling hard on the cord.

"I cannot take the belt off,"
Meowth told Pikachu. "Jessie has
the only key."

Pikachu was angry. It pulled

harder on the cord. Meowth
pulled hard, too. They tried to get
away from each other. But the
cord did not break. They were
still stuck together.

"*Pik-a-chuuu!*" yelled the
Electric Pokémon. It blasted
Meowth.

"Okay, okay," said Meowth. "You
win. I will go your way."

Pikachu led the way. Meowth
followed. It walked on one side of
a tree. Pikachu walked on the
other side of the tree. The cord
wrapped around the tree and

stopped them both.

"You come around this way, Pikachu," said Meowth.

Pikachu's cheeks began to spark.

"Fine. I will come around," said Meowth quickly.

"*Pika,*" said Pikachu. Ash's Pokémon did not want any more trouble from Meowth.

"It is not easy to be the weak one," Meowth sulked. But suddenly,

it thought of a plan!

*I will be nice to Pikachu,* Meowth thought. *I will pretend to bring Pikachu to its friends. Then I will lead it to the boss.*

"I have been thinking, Pikachu," said Meowth in its sweetest voice. "We should be friends. As a favor, I will take you back to your trainer. Just follow me."

But Pikachu did not believe Meowth. It could tell Meowth was up to no good! "*Pik-a-chuuu!*" it cried. Then Pikachu shocked Meowth again.

"*Pika pika, pi!*" yelled Pikachu. *You cannot fool me, Meowth!*

"You knew I was trying to trick you?" asked Meowth shakily.

"*Pika pi.*" Pikachu gave Meowth a hard look. *Do not try that again!*

Meowth sighed. It knew it could not trick Pikachu. It would have to behave.

# CHAPTER FIVE

## Working Together

Meowth followed along after Pikachu. The two Pokémon wanted to find their trainers. They began searching for them.

But then, Pikachu stopped. "What are you doing?" Meowth asked.

"*Pika pika pi,*" Pikachu

sniffed. *I smell something.*

"I do not smell anything," said
Meowth. Then it remembered,
"Oh, yeah, I do not have a nose."

"*Pika!*" cried Pikachu. *Look
out!*

Meowth
looked up.
A giant
Rhydon was
looking down
at them.

"AHHH!"
cried Meowth. Its knees were
shaking.

"*Pika! Pika!*" cried Pikachu. *Run, Meowth!* But Meowth was so scared it could not move.

Pikachu ran fast. *Bump, bump, bump* went Meowth behind it.

"Thank you, Pikachu," Meowth said. "That was close."

But Rhydon was still chasing them. Pikachu ran one way. Meowth ran the other way. *Snap!* The cord pulled them back together.

Rhydon roared. It was getting closer!

Meowth raced over a cliff.

Pikachu tumbled after it. Down the rocks charged Rhydon.

The Pokémon ran fast, but they were trapped. They had run into a dead end!

"*Pika! Pikachu!*" cried Pikachu. *We must fight it!*

"We have to fight?" cried Meowth. "It is too big!"

"*Pik-a-chuuu!*" Pikachu sent an Electric Blast at Rhydon. But Rhydon had thick skin. The attack did not work.

"*Pika pikachu,*" said Pikachu. *We must work together.*

"What can *I* do?" asked Meowth.

"*Pika pika pi!*" Pikachu explained the plan.

"Okay," agreed Meowth. "I will do it."

"*Rhydon!*" thundered Rhydon. It was coming closer. Meowth and Pikachu waited till it was very near. Then they leaped — onto its head! Meowth tickled the giant Pokémon. It opened its mouth to laugh.

"*Pikachuuu!*" Pikachu sent a Thunder Wave right into Rhydon's open mouth!

27

*Bam!* The huge Pokémon
fainted and fell to the ground.

"We did it!" cried Meowth.

"*Pika!*" cheered Pikachu. The
two Pokémon grinned at each
other. They had worked as a
team!

# CHAPTER SIX

## The Search

On another part of the island, Marill was helping Ash look for Pikachu. Tracey's Pokémon was good at tracking. It soon found a Pidgeot's nest on top of a cliff. Ash climbed the rocks.

"*Pidgeot!*" screamed a giant Pidgeot. It did not want Ash near

its nest. *Swoop!* The giant
Pidgeot knocked Ash off the cliff.

"Are you okay?" Misty asked.
"Was Pikachu there?"

"No," said Ash. "I must find it."

Marill wanted to help. It
listened for another Pidgeot.

"Ash really
cares about
Pikachu,"
said Tracey.

"Yes," agreed
Misty, "and Pikachu loves Ash.
They are a great team."

All day the group searched for

Pikachu. "Pikachu!" Ash called again and again.

Marill turned its ears to listen for Pikachu, but it did not hear anything.

"*Togi! Togi!*" cried Togepi. It was excited. It pointed to footprints in the mud.

"Those are Pikachu's footprints!" cried Ash.

"And Meowth's," said Tracey. "And a giant Rhydon's!"

"Pikachu cannot fight a Rhydon that size," said Misty.

Misty and Togepi looked at Ash. He was very worried.

"Please be okay, Pikachu," Ash whispered.

———

Jessie and James were looking for Pikachu and Meowth, too. They were looking from above, from their hot air balloon.

"Have you spotted them, James?" Jessie asked.

"Nope," said James.

"That Meowth is more work than it's worth," Jessie grumbled.

# CHAPTER SEVEN

## Sharing

It was evening. Pikachu and
Meowth were tired of walking.

"I am so hungry," said Meowth.

"*Pika,*" agreed Pikachu sadly.

Suddenly, their eyes lit up!
There was an apple hanging from
a tree right in front of them!

Meowth ran. Pikachu ran. Who

would get there first?

Meowth jumped for the apple. But Pikachu pulled the cord, and Meowth fell down.

"*Pika!*" Pikachu said with a smile. It sent an Electric Shock up, and the apple tumbled down — right to Pikachu.

Poor Meowth! Its eyes started to water. Pikachu felt sorry for the other Pokémon. It had been a long day for both of them.

Pikachu broke the apple in half. "*Pikachu,*" it said. *Here you go.*

Meowth could not believe it.

"You are giving this to *me*?"

Pikachu nodded.

"No one is ever nice to Meowth," said Meowth sadly.

Pikachu smiled at Meowth. It was happy to share.

"Thank you," Meowth said, eating its apple. Now it smiled, too. "This is delicious."

Meowth looked at Pikachu. It remembered all the times that Pikachu had shocked it. But Pikachu had just been

protecting itself. It was not a bad Pokémon.

Suddenly, Meowth had an idea. "Join Team Rocket, Pikachu!" it cried. "We will be great friends. Look at how well we work together!"

But Pikachu did not answer. It was fast asleep.

"Oh, well," said Meowth to its new friend. "Good night, Pikachu."

# CHAPTER EIGHT

## The Battle

The next morning, Pikachu and Meowth woke up to a loud noise. It was Pidgeot screeching.

"Not again!" cried Meowth.

"*Pika!*" cried Pikachu. *Run!*

The Pokémon ran from Pidgeot as fast as they could.

Then, suddenly, they heard

another scary noise.

"*Rhydon.*" It was Rhydon. And it was coming after them, too!

The little Pokémon huddled together. They did not know what to do. The giant Pokémon were attacking from both sides.

"Pikachu!" a voice cried.

Pikachu looked up. It was Ash!

At the same time, Meowth saw Jessie and James. They were in a hot air balloon.

"Go, Snorlax!" cried Ash.

Snorlax came out of the Poké Ball. It looked like a teddy bear.

But it was very big.

"Stop Rhydon!" shouted Ash.
He had to rescue Pikachu!

Pidgeot was getting closer.

"Go, Arbok!" called Jessie.

"Snorlax, Megapunch!" ordered
Ash.

Snorlax hurled a giant punch at
the giant Rhydon. It fainted. At
the same time, Arbok went after
Pidgeot. With a screech, it flew
away.

"Not bad," said Jessie.

"Way to go, Snorlax," said Ash.

# CHAPTER NINE

## Freedom

"Jessie! James!" cried Meowth. It ran to Team Rocket. Pikachu went *bump, bump, bump* behind.

"Thank you for finding me. You must have looked all night!" Meowth cried happily.

"No," said Jessie. "We were trying to catch a Rhydon. We

found you by
mistake."

"Oh," sighed
Meowth.

*Bump, bump,
bump.* Pikachu was
running now,
dragging Meowth behind it. Ash
held his arms out. Pikachu ran
into them.

"Pikachu!" Ash cried. "We
looked everywhere! Are you
okay?"

"*Pika pika,*" said Pikachu. It
was happy to see Ash.

Misty and Tracey were glad, too. Even little Togepi squeaked happily.

Then Team Rocket pulled on Meowth's arms. They were trying to get Pikachu away from Ash.

"You are hurting me!" yelled Meowth.

Ash pulled hard on the cord. James held tight.

"Go, Bulbasaur!" yelled Ash.

"Go, Arbok!" cried Jessie.

"Pikachu!" called Ash, lifting up his Pokémon. Pikachu sent a Thunder Wave right at Arbok.

"Go, Victreebel!" said James as Arbok fainted.

Now the two Plant Pokémon began to battle. They got too close to Jessie. She was so scared, she dropped the key to Pikachu's belt.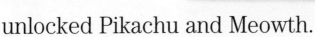

"I got it!" cried Ash. Quickly he unlocked Pikachu and Meowth.

"Now you are free!" he said, hugging Pikachu.

# CHAPTER TEN

## Together Again

Bulbasaur chased Team Rocket back to their balloon. "We will get Pikachu back!" shouted Meowth. "Prepare to attack!"

Misty shook her head.

"They just cannot get enough!" she said. "Go, Staryu!"

But instead of Staryu, Psyduck

appeared. "Oh, no! Not you again, Psyduck!" Misty cried. "Oh, well. Send them flying with your Confusion Attack!"

But before Psyduck could attack, something strange happened.

"*Togi, togi,*" squealed Togepi. It squirmed in Misty's arms.

"Blast off!" cried Meowth. The hot air balloon rose into the air.

Togepi raised its little arms. It

looked at Team Rocket.

*Boom!* The balloon burst in the sky.

"Looks like Team Rocket is blasting off again!" cried Jessie, James, and Meowth. Team Rocket disappeared far, far away.

"*Togepi!*" said Misty's little Pokémon happily.

"Psyduck did not make that attack," said Tracey.

"*Togi, togi,*" squealed Togepi.

Misty looked at her little Pokémon with wonder.

"Could it have been Togepi?

Did you do that?" Misty asked.

"*Brrrr! Togi!*" it cried.

Misty hugged her little Pokémon.

Ash was hugging Pikachu, too.

"You had me worried," Ash said, lifting Pikachu up into the air.

"You and Pikachu are a great match, Ash," said Misty.

"*Pika.*" Pikachu smiled. It was happy to be back with its friends!

# All aboard the Pokémon Showboat!

## Chapter Book #6:
## Raichu Shows Off

Ash and Pikachu set sail aboard a ship of performing Pokémon. They make friends with a Raichu and its trainer, Kay. But when Team Rocket tries to steal the show, Pikachu, Ash and their new friends must make 'em walk the plank! Can they save the ship in time?

**Coming soon to a bookstore near you!**

Visit us at www.scholastic.com

■SCHOLASTIC

POKJR999